SWAN COVE

By JANE WHITE CANFIELD

Pictures by JO POLSENO

An Early I CAN READ Book

HARPER & ROW, PUBLISHERS
New York, Hagerstown, San Francisco, London

Swan Cove
Text copyright © 1978 by Jane White Canfield
Illustrations copyright © 1978 by Jo Polseno
All rights reserved. No part of this book may be used or
reproduced in any manner whatsoever without written
permission except in the case of brief quotations embodied
in critical articles and reviews. Printed in the United
States of America. For information address Harper & Row,
Publishers, Inc., 10 East 53rd Street, New York, N.Y. 10022.
Published simultaneously in Canada by Fitzhenry & Whiteside
Limited, Toronto.
First Edition

Library of Congress Cataloging in Publication Data
Canfield, Jane White.
    Swan cove.

    (An Early I can read book)
    SUMMARY: A quiet cove on a small island is the
summer home for a pair of swans and their offspring.
    [1. Swans—Fiction]   I. Polseno, Jo.   II. Title.
PZ10.3.C164Sw   [E]   77-11832
ISBN 0-06-020948-8
ISBN 0-06-020949-6 lib. bdg.

*To Eliza
who lives on
Swan Cove*

In a cove on a small island

off the coast of Connecticut

live two swans,

the male, the cob,

the female, the pen.

It is their home in the summers.

Along the banks of the cove
there are beech trees,
bullrushes and berry bushes.
At one end there is an inlet.

6

A small spit of land

protects the cove

from ocean storms.

There are frogs and fish,

a family of muskrats,

and ducks and gulls.

The swans eat the grass and
juicy weeds that grow
on the edge of the cove
and under the water.

Very early in the spring

the cob and pen mate.

Swans mate for life.

They swim close together,

dip their heads in the water,

raise their necks

and touch their beaks.

Then the cob

grabs the pen by the neck

and gets up on her back.

10

Soon they choose a safe place

and begin to build a nest.

The place must be near the water.

It must be high,

away from danger.

11

They build together.

The cob plucks the grass and twigs

with his beak.

He tosses them over his back

to the pen.

She makes the nest around her.

It takes a long time to build.

The pen lays four eggs.

The pen and cob take turns

sitting on the eggs.

If danger comes

they flap their wings

and hiss loudly.

After many days

the eggs begin to hatch.

The pen and the cob

take great care of the baby cygnets.

But one day

two black-backed gulls

attack the cygnets.

Only one little cygnet

lives through the summer.

He grows big and strong.

His brown feathers

slowly turn white.

The happy family

swims around in safety.

One day a stranger-cob

and a stranger-pen

swim into the cove

with their two cygnets.

They want to live in

this very special place too.

At once the cob

swims out to the strangers.

This is *his* home.

The two pens

with their cygnets

stand on the bank.

They are very excited.

The two cobs begin to fight.

They flap their wings!

They splash!

They hiss!

Round and round they fight

like two prize-fighters.

Slowly the stranger-cob

begins to grow weak.

The cob holds him under water.

The stranger-cob has lost.

The stranger-pen takes her two cygnets

and swims quickly

for the inlet and the sea.

Her drooping cob

follows slowly.

The cob swims after them.

He flaps his wings,

stretches out his neck,

and hisses until

the strangers are out of sight.

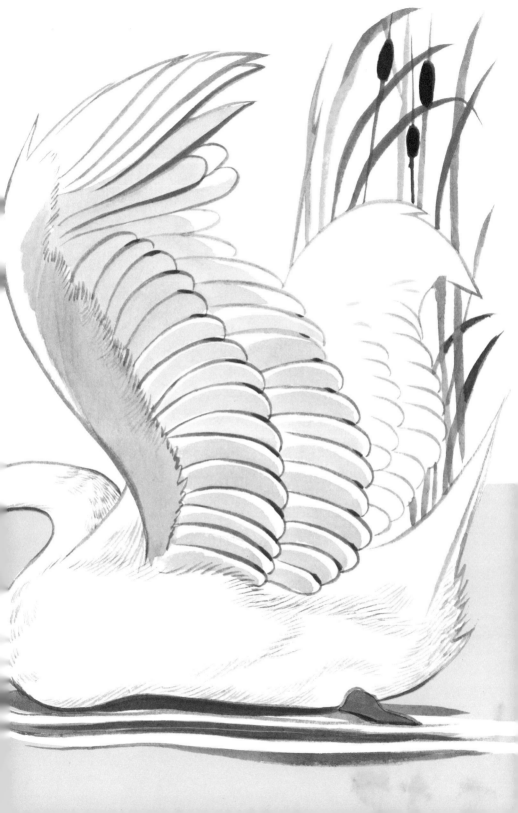

Then he stands

high up on the sand spit

and spreads his wings.

He holds his head high.

He is the winner.

His pen with their cygnet

swims out to meet him.

She mounts on his back.

She puts her wings around him

and preens and strokes his neck.

He is her brave cob.

For the rest of the summer

the swan family live in peace

in their cove

off the coast of Connecticut.